P9-CLU-212

Children's Treasury

Cover illustrated by Emma Pearce

Copyright © 2013 Publications International, Ltd. All rights reserved.

This publication may not be reproduced in whole or in part by
any means whatsoever without written permission from

Louis Weber, C.E.O., Publications International, Ltd.
7373 North Cicero Avenue   Ground Floor, 59 Gloucester Place
Lincolnwood, Illinois 60712   London W1U 8JJ

Permission is never granted for commercial purposes.

Customer Service: 1-800-595-8484 or customer_service@pilbooks.com

www.pilbooks.com

p i kids is a trademark of Publications International, Ltd.,
and is registered in the United States.

8 7 6 5 4 3 2 1

ISBN-13: 978-1-4508-5159-6
ISBN-10: 1-4508-5159-2

Children's Treasury

Collection of Favorite Stories

pi kids® publications international, ltd.

Contents

Gulliver's Travels

Adapted from the story by Jonathan Swift
Illustrated by Karen Stormer Brooks

here once was a man named Gulliver who longed for adventure. One day he set out on a journey to explore distant lands. Not long into the voyage, a horrible storm struck. The crew was tossed from the ship and the waves swallowed them. They were lost at sea.

Gulliver awoke on a grassy shore. He could not move, but he felt something walking up his leg and onto his chest. When he peered down at his body, he saw tiny humans no bigger than spoons standing on his chest.

He tried to lift his head, but found that his whole body had been tied down with fine ropes. With a little effort, the ropes broke, and Gulliver sat up. The little people began to panic, so Gulliver stayed very still. Soon the little people understood that he didn't want to harm them.

The emperor of the little people stood on a platform and spoke to Gulliver in a language that Gulliver could not understand. Patiently, Gulliver waited for the little man to end his speech.

When the emperor was finished, Gulliver smiled and pointed to his mouth. The little man saw that Gulliver was hungry, and ordered his subjects to serve him enough food for 200 people.

After he ate, the people brought a specially made cart. Gulliver climbed aboard and 900 little people pulled him to their capital city.

Gulliver was excited to learn about this strange land, called Lilliput, and its people. He worked very hard to understand their language and to discover as much as he could about their interesting culture and customs.

The Lilliputians were fascinated with their visitor. Gulliver showed them his few possessions that had survived the storm: coins, a pen, and his pocket watch. The Lilliputians were most interested in how the watch ticked and what it was used to measure.

Gulliver enjoyed his time with the Lilliputians, and they loved to entertain him. One day he saw the army of Lilliput practicing their drills. They looked just like Gulliver's toy soldiers from when he was a boy.

In a nearby field Gulliver made a stage out of his handkerchief and placed all of the soldiers and horses on it. Then he lifted the emperor up in his hand to watch the army's drills from above. The emperor was so impressed, he wanted all Lilliputians to see the army practice each day.

A few weeks later, the emperor told Gulliver that the Lilliputians were getting ready for battle. For a very long time they had been at war with the only other kingdom they knew, an island nation called Blefuscu.

The emperor of Lilliput and the emperor of Blefuscu bickered over which end of an egg is best to crack first. The emperor of Blefuscu claimed it was the small end, while the emperor of Lilliput declared it was the large end. Each one knew his way was best, and the argument turned into a war.

The Lilliputians had a fine army, but they did not have a navy or any battleships. The emperor asked for Gulliver's help.

Gulliver's job during the battle would be to stop the ships from Blefuscu before they arrived on the shores of Lilliput.

Gulliver set out on his own across the sea. He soon met the enemy ships as they left the shores of Blefuscu. By simply rising out of the water, Gulliver frightened the Blefuscudians terribly. Most of them dove from their ships and swam back to shore.

Some soldiers shot arrows from their ships, but Gulliver brushed them off like little thorns.

Gulliver tugged the Blefuscudian ships across the sea to the land of Lilliput. Great cheers rose from the shore as he came closer, pulling the entire fleet of Blefuscu with one massive hand! Without their battleships, the people of Blefuscu could no longer wage war against the Lilliputians.

From that day forward, the little people of Lilliput called Gulliver the greatest warrior of all time. He had ended many sad years of battle.

One day, Gulliver spotted a ship out at sea just like the one he had sailed on. It was time for him to go. The emperor of Lilliput gave Gulliver several cows and some food for his journey. Then he thanked Gulliver for all of his help.

Gulliver was welcomed aboard the passing ship. He told the crew about his voyage to Lilliput. No one believed his story until he reached into his pocket and pulled out the tiny cattle he had received from the emperor. That was more than enough to convince them!

On the next leg of his journey, Gulliver's ship sailed into a monsoon and was tossed about for days. Gulliver swam to a nearby shore for help.

Next to the shore Gulliver found a field of tall grass. Each blade of grass was taller than three people! Soon Gulliver felt the ground shake, and he was nearly squashed by a massive shoe.

The shoe belonged to a giant farmer who saw Gulliver and picked him up. With an amazed laugh and a big grin, the farmer dropped Gulliver into the darkness of his shirt pocket.

The farmer thought he might show the little man to his friends in town. His friends were amazed with what they saw. To them, Gulliver was only the size of a doll, but he walked and talked like everyone else.

Soon everyone in town wanted to see the living doll. The farmer set up a booth at the market. The townspeople gave the farmer money for the chance to see Gulliver. The farmer told Gulliver to sing and dance as the crowds of people lined up in the streets to see him.

Soon the queen heard about the fascinating little man and went to see him. She was very amused with Gulliver, and bought the little man from the farmer for a great sum of money.

Gulliver was very comfortable at the palace inside the tiny room that the queen had made for him. But Gulliver was only allowed to leave the room when the queen asked for him. She called for him at least once a day, at dinner. Gulliver ate at the queen's table. She and her court enjoyed watching him while they dined.

Gulliver soon grew weary of his life in the palace. He spent each day stuck in his room, waiting for the queen to call on him. The queen didn't like to see Gulliver sad, so she ordered her servants to carry him out on walks around the palace grounds each day.

The queen also learned that Gulliver had once been a sailor. She had a tiny sailboat built especially for him. After dinner, the queen and her subjects gathered around the fountain to watch Gulliver practice his sailing skills.

The king, however, became bored with just one tiny man, so he put Gulliver in a box and sent him with his men to search the shore for little people.

On the shore, an eagle swooped down and picked up Gulliver's box. It carried him over the ocean and dropped him in the water. A while later, Gulliver's box was found by a passing ship. The crew rescued him, and he shared his stories from his adventures as they sailed back home. Everyone was enthralled with Gulliver's tales of Lilliput and the land of giants, and his stories lived on forever.

The Velveteen Rabbit

Adapted from the story by Margery Williams
Illustrated by Elena Kucharik

ne Christmas morning, a very excited boy couldn't wait to go downstairs and see what Santa had brought him.

His stocking held a wonderful surprise: a velveteen rabbit. The boy kissed and squeezed the rabbit and held it under his arm for the entire day.

The boy's nursery was filled with many fancy toys, which made the velveteen rabbit feel very plain. The only toy in the nursery who became friends with the velveteen rabbit was an old horse.

"Fancy toys don't last," said the horse. "They don't have anything lovable inside of them. Fancy toys will never become real."

"What does it mean to be real?" asked the velveteen rabbit.

"You become real after someone loves you for a long, long time," answered the old horse.

That night the boy's nanny couldn't find the toy dog that the boy usually held while he slept.

"He'll help you get to sleep tonight," said the nanny as she handed the boy the velveteen rabbit.

The boy took the velveteen rabbit and held him tight. The soft rabbit fit the crook of the boy's arm just right, and the boy quickly fell asleep.

The velveteen rabbit loved being held and hugged by the boy. For the whole night, the velveteen rabbit felt very special, and he hoped that the boy would love him for a very long time.

From that night on, the velveteen rabbit looked forward to bedtime, when the boy would hug him as he fell asleep. But the two also spent their days together. The boy loved the velveteen rabbit so much that he took him everywhere he went. The velveteen rabbit's heart was filled with joy. He loved the boy and felt very lucky.

The rabbit was so happy, he didn't notice how shabby he had become. His fur was dirty from days spent outside, and the space between his ears was wearing thin from being petted.

One afternoon the boy left the velveteen rabbit hiding in the garden while he went to pick berries. When it began to rain, the boy ran inside and forgot about his dear velveteen rabbit.

At bedtime, the boy realized that he had left his friend out in the rain and begged his nanny to go find him.

"That's the last time I go out in the rain for a toy!" said the nanny, handing the boy his rabbit.

"He is not a toy! He's real!" shouted the boy.

This made the velveteen rabbit very happy.

One day the boy placed the velveteen rabbit by a tree while he went to play. After he left, two strange creatures arrived. They looked like toy rabbits, but they could hop all by themselves.

"Would you like to come and play with us?" asked one of the rabbits.

"No, thank you," said the velveteen rabbit.

"He's not real. He's just a toy!" said the other rabbit as they hopped away.

The velveteen rabbit remembered what the old horse had said, and longed to be real.

Before long the velveteen rabbit forgot about the two rabbits in the woods. He was too busy spending time with the boy.

One day the boy became very ill. While he was sick, the velveteen rabbit worried about him. He stayed close to the boy and did whatever he could to help him get better.

The velveteen rabbit spent his days whispering to the boy about all the fun they would have when he was well again. The velveteen rabbit was sure he could make the boy feel better.

With the help of the velveteen rabbit, the boy soon got better. Then the boy went on vacation and accidentally left the velveteen rabbit behind.

The velveteen rabbit began to cry. In the spot where his tears had fallen, a flower grew. The flower held a magical fairy who said, "Your love for the boy has earned you the right to become real!"

Suddenly the rabbit could hop on his own.

"Wasn't I real before?" asked the rabbit.

"Only to the boy," answered the fairy. "Now you are real to everyone!"

The Brave Little Tailor

Illustrated by Jeremy Tugeau

ne morning a little tailor was sewing in his shop, looking forward to a snack of bread and jam.

When a swarm of flies began to buzz around his food, the little tailor shooed them away with his hands, but the flies kept coming back.

The tailor grabbed a scrap of cloth and slapped it down onto the buzzing flies. When he lifted the cloth, seven flies lay dead on the table.

"Seven flies in one blow!" said the tailor. "The whole world should know of my victory!"

So the tailor decided to go on an adventure to tell the world of his skill. Before he left, he looked for useful things to take with him. All he could find was a piece of cheese. When he left his house he found a bird stuck in the bushes. The tailor freed the bird and put it in his pocket with the cheese.

The tailor walked through town and up the side of a mountain. At the top, he met a giant.

"Hello, Giant," said the tailor. "I am on a great adventure. Will you join me?"

"A little man like you on a great adventure?" the giant laughed.

"But I've killed seven in one blow!" said the tailor, who was very proud.

The giant thought the tailor meant seven men, not flies. He found it very hard to believe that this little tailor could kill seven in one blow.

The giant decided to test the little tailor's strength. "Can you do this?" asked the giant. He picked up a stone and crushed it with his hands.

The tailor was not as strong as the giant, but he was very clever. The tailor took the cheese from his pocket and crushed it into liquid whey.

"Can you do this?" asked the giant. He picked up a stone and threw it up in the air, out of sight.

"Watch this," said the tailor, as he took the bird out of his pocket. With a toss of his hand, the bird flew fast out of sight.

The giant, who was not very smart, didn't know that the tailor had used a piece of cheese and a bird instead of stones in his feats of strength. Dumbfounded by the strong little tailor, the giant decided to test him one more time.

"If you are so strong," said the giant, "help me carry this tree."

"Of course," said the tailor, "I will carry the branches. I wouldn't want them to scratch you!"

When the giant picked up the trunk, the tailor rode on the branches, fooling the giant again.

The giant returned home and told his friends about the little tailor who had killed seven in one blow, and could squeeze rocks into water, throw stones into the heavens, and carry trees.

The tailor, who had followed the giant, overheard the giant's story and walked over to greet him and his friends. All of the giants fled in fear of the strong and mighty tailor.

Word of the brave tailor, who had killed seven in one blow and could make giants flee, reached the king, who asked the little tailor for a big favor.

There were two more mischievous giants living in the king's woods. The king told the tailor that if he could get rid of the giants, he could have the princess's hand in marriage.

So the tailor went into the woods and found the two giants sleeping under a tree. He climbed the tree and dropped acorns on their heads.

"Why did you wake me by thumping my head?" roared one of the giants. The giants began to quarrel, and then fought each other until they both lay dead under the tree.

The king was very happy to hear of the tailor's victory over the giants, and asked the tailor for one more favor: to capture a dangerous wild unicorn.

The tailor agreed, and set off to find the wild unicorn. As he entered a nearby village, the tailor saw the unicorn charging toward him. The tailor stood by a tree and stayed very still. At the last minute, he jumped out of the way.

The unicorn's horn stuck fast into the tree's trunk. The tailor freed the unicorn, then rode it back to the king's palace and married the princess.

No one ever knew that the brave prince was really just a clever little tailor, but the princess was suspicious of his origins.

One night in his sleep the princess heard him mumble, "This new fabric would make a fine waistcoat!"

The princess tried to listen closer, but the clever tailor quickly realized what he had said and continued, "After all, a brave prince who can kill seven in one blow should have the finest waistcoat in the kingdom, should he not?"

A Story for Squeakins

Illustrated by Teri Weidner

It was time for little Squeakins to take his afternoon nap, so he asked old Granny Mouse to read him a story. Stories always helped Squeakins fall asleep.

"Alright then, dearest dear," said Granny. "What kind of a story would you like to hear?"

"A nice one, with a happy ending," answered Squeakins.

So Granny went to fetch the happiest-ending storybook she could find. But on her way to the library, she ran into a bit of trouble. The trouble was mean old Mittens the cat, guarding the door.

"Hello, Granny," said mean old Mittens. "What a nice treat you'd be to eat."

"Oh, no! You must let me pass," said Granny Mouse. "I must fetch a happy-ending story to read to Squeakins before his nap."

"Well," said Mittens, "I'll let you pass if you promise to bring me fresh milk from the cow."

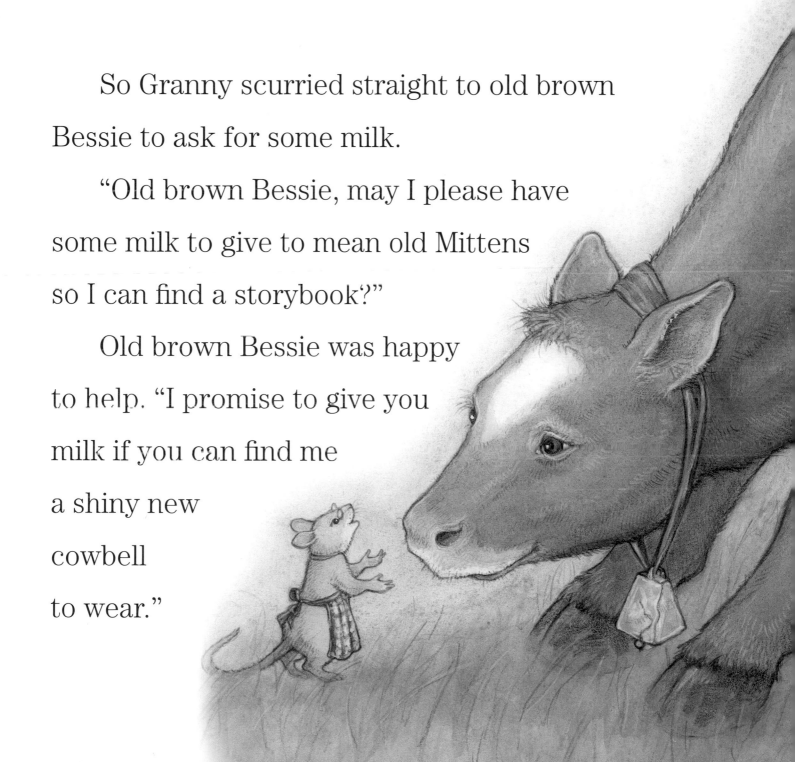

So Granny scurried straight to old brown Bessie to ask for some milk.

"Old brown Bessie, may I please have some milk to give to mean old Mittens so I can find a storybook?"

Old brown Bessie was happy to help. "I promise to give you milk if you can find me a shiny new cowbell to wear."

So Granny Mouse scurried straight to old tinker Tom to ask him for a shiny new cowbell. "Old tinker Tom, may I please have a shiny new cowbell for old brown Bessie?" asked Granny Mouse. "I must fetch a happy storybook for Squeakins!"

"I will give you a cowbell, if you make me a glass of lemonade," said tinker Tom.

So Granny scurried to the leafy old lemon tree to ask for some lemons to make lemonade.

"Leafy old lemon tree, may I please have some round yellow lemons to make a glass of lemonade for old tinker Tom so he will give old brown Bessie a shiny new cowbell so that she will give fresh milk to mean old Mittens so I can pass? I must find a happy story to read to Squeakins."

"I'll give you as many lemons as you like," said the leafy old lemon tree, "if you can find some water to sprinkle on me."

So Granny Mouse stood in the middle of the yard to talk to the clouds. "Puffy, fluffy clouds, may I please have some water to sprinkle on the old leafy lemon tree so he will give me lemons to make lemonade for old tinker Tom...."

Granny took a breath. "So that old tinker Tom will give me a shiny new cowbell for old brown Bessie so that she will give me fresh milk for mean old Mittens so I can pass?" asked dear Granny Mouse. "Because I must fetch a happy-ending storybook for Squeakins!"

And the puffy, fluffy clouds answered Granny Mouse with a big "*BOOM!*" and it began to rain on the leafy old lemon tree.

Well! What do you think happened next?

The clouds gave water.

The tree gave lemons.

Old tinker Tom gave a cowbell.

Old brown Bessie gave milk.

And mean old Mittens let Granny pass.

Finally, Granny fetched the happiest-ending storybook that she could find to read to little Squeakins. But by the time Granny got back… he was already asleep!

King Midas

Illustrated by Jeff Pike

There once was a king named Midas who was very rich, but he was also very greedy. King Midas spent every day locked away in his vault counting his riches. There was nothing that King Midas loved more than adding up his precious treasures.

King Midas had a beautiful daughter named Marygold. Marygold preferred to spend her days outdoors tending to the flowers in the palace garden. There was nothing Marygold loved more than the smell of beautiful roses.

Every day, Marygold asked her father to visit her garden, but he refused to come outside. He was much too busy counting his glorious gold.

One day as King Midas counted the gold in his vault, a mysterious stranger appeared. The stranger told King Midas that he could give him the power to make everything he touched turn to glistening gold.

Greedy Midas could not believe his ears. "Yes! Yes! I want the power to turn everything to gold!"

"Very well," said the stranger. "After sunrise, anything you touch will turn to gold."

When the dawn's light finally appeared, King Midas reached to draw back the curtain, and it turned into solid gold! He ran from room to room touching everything he could reach—tables, mirrors, candlesticks, paintings, and doors. Just like the mysterious stranger had promised, everything turned to gold.

"I have the magical touch of gold!" shouted the king.

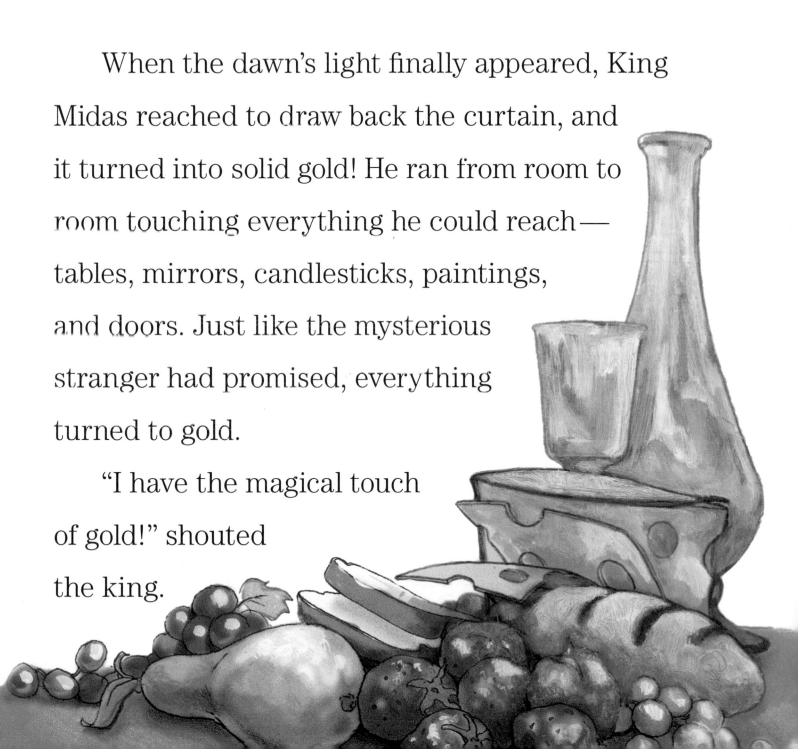

King Midas rushed from his castle to Marygold's garden, where he found her beautiful flowers. He laid his hands on one of her loveliest roses, and it turned from scarlet red to gold.

"How delighted Marygold will be when she finds her flowers turned to gold!" said the king as he continued to touch all the flowers in her garden.

Marygold saw what her father was doing and begged him to stop. "How could you let this happen to my beautiful flowers?" she sobbed.

"Please don't be sad, Marygold," said the king. "Now you have the most beautiful flowers in the world because they are gold!"

Marygold still sobbed. The king comforted her by hugging her, but the hug turned Marygold to gold!

King Midas was shocked at what had become of Marygold. His new power had turned into a curse instead of a blessing.

The mysterious stranger appeared again. "How do you like your new power?" he asked.

"I loathe it," King Midas answered. "I'll give you all of my gold if you can change everything back to the way it was before."

"I do not want your gold," said the stranger. "I only wanted to teach you a lesson. Tomorrow everything will be as it was."

The stranger disappeared, and the next morning, just as he had said, everything was the way it had been. From that day forward King Midas only spent his time doing things that really mattered, especially helping Marygold with her garden.

The Brownie
Of Blednock

Illustrated by Gwen Connelly

 t was a quiet day in the village of Blednock when everyone heard a soft humming sound. As the humming got louder, the villagers lined the streets to find its source. The hum, it seemed, was coming from a little man walking straight into Blednock.

As the little man approached, the villagers fell silent. They had never seen anything like him!

"Any work for Aiken-Drum? Any work for Aiken-Drum?" the little man asked.

What was Aiken-Drum? No one seemed to know. The people were more curious than ever, so they gathered around their new visitor.

Then Granny, the wisest woman in town, had something to say. "I think Aiken-Drum is what our visitor calls himself," she announced. "I believe he is a brownie."

"Yes, I am a brownie," said the little man. "And I would like to work for the people of Blednock."

The brownie continued, "If I am to work here, you must understand that the ways of my people are very different from yours. In our land, we work only to make people happy, never for money or possessions. All I require is a place to sleep and something warm to drink at bedtime."

"I've heard that brownies are the best workers," Granny told her neighbors, "and if there's a town that needs a helping hand, it's Blednock!"

Granny took the brownie to the blacksmith, who agreed to let Aiken-Drum sleep in his barn. He gave the brownie a simple horse's blanket on a bed of fresh hay.

The blacksmith, who had met many brownies in his days, did not bring food or fancy pillows and blankets to Aiken-Drum. He knew that would anger the brownie, and he didn't want to upset the little man who had traveled so far to make people happy. By keeping his lodging plain, the blacksmith respected the brownie's wishes.

At the end of each day, Granny brought the brownie something warm to drink. She too remembered Aiken-Drum's simple needs.

The townspeople loved to spot the brownie working, but he did most of his work at night.

Every morning, the blacksmith found the brownie's mug empty, and the blanket folded neatly in a corner. He was always out working.

Soon, all of the people of Blednock were sharing stories about the magical work of the brownie. Everyone was very grateful.

Old Mother Jones reported that the brownie had cleaned her whole house and made her a pot of porridge for breakfast.

The farmer told everyone about how the brownie led all of his sheep to the safety of the barn just before a sudden summer storm.

More and more stories were being told of the good work that Aiken-Drum had been doing in Blednock. The town was looking better than it ever had because of its new visitor. Anytime that work needed to be done, Aiken-Drum was there.

The children of Blednock loved to play with Aiken-Drum. Each day they crowded around the brownie, giggling and asking him to play games.

"Tell us a story, Aiken-Drum."

"Teach us a song, Aiken-Drum."

"Show us a dance, Aiken-Drum."

Aiken-Drum would start a bonfire and tell stories and play with the children until their parents called them in for dinner. When the children went off to their houses, Aiken-Drum went back to work.

Everyone thought things around Blednock were better than ever, except for Miss Daisy Fain. "I think things are unfair in this village. It's not right to let a brownie work so hard for so little."

A neighbor disagreed. "Aiken-Drum believes that work should only be done for the joy of making other people happy. He made it plain that he does not want money or possessions."

But Miss Daisy didn't believe her neighbor, and she decided to repay Aiken-Drum for his hard work by making him a new pair of trousers.

That night Aiken-Drum returned to the barn and saw the new trousers resting on his bed of hay. He knew that someone was trying to pay him, and he became very sad. His new friends had not respected his wish to be paid in simple kindness. He disappeared that very night.

The next morning the villagers searched far and wide for their friend, but he was nowhere to be found. No one knew why he had left...except for Miss Daisy Fain, who never disrespected the wishes of her friends from that day forward.

The Emperor's New Clothes

Illustrated by John Kanzler

Once upon a time there was an emperor who loved clothes more than anything else. He selected the finest fabrics ever seen, and hired the most talented tailors in his kingdom.

Word of the emperor who loved fine clothes reached two thieves in a faraway land. They thought of a brilliant plan. "We can use the emperor's love of fine clothes to make ourselves rich!" said one thief. "And we'll never have to sew a single stitch!"

The sneaky thieves introduced themselves to the emperor as expert tailors.

The thieves told the emperor that their fabric was made from the finest strands of thread in all the world, and that it was magical.

"Only the wisest people in the land will see the magical fabric," they said. "It will be invisible to fools and simpletons."

The thieves opened their bag and carefully lifted something into the air. They held up their arms before the emperor.

The emperor squinted. He saw nothing in their hands! Was he a fool? The emperor was embarrassed, so he said, "That is the most fantastic, beautiful fabric I have ever seen!"

The emperor ordered clothes made from the thieves' magical fabric, and he sent a royal servant to check on their work. The servant was stunned by what he didn't see. The tailors were weaving, cutting, and sewing fabric that was not there. Was he a fool? He could never let the emperor know.

After many weeks, the thieves brought the emperor his new clothes. The emperor was sure the clothes were beautiful, even though he could not see them. He put the clothes on slowly, careful not to tear the tailors' expert stitching. Dressed in his new clothes, he had never felt more dashing.

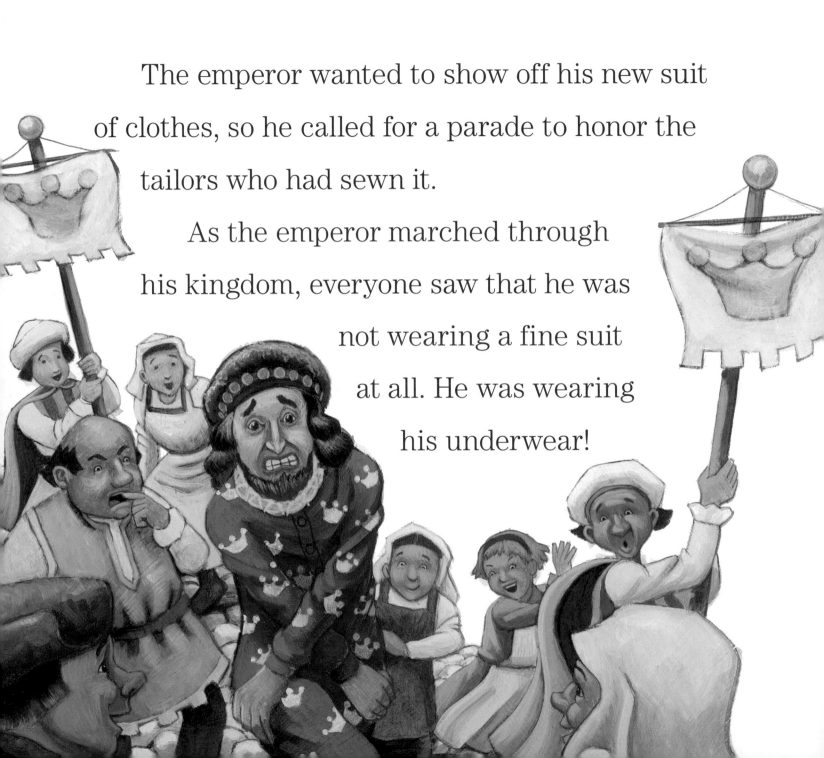

The emperor wanted to show off his new suit of clothes, so he called for a parade to honor the tailors who had sewn it.

As the emperor marched through his kingdom, everyone saw that he was not wearing a fine suit at all. He was wearing his underwear!

Everyone was afraid to tell the emperor, except for one small child. "Why isn't the emperor wearing any clothes?" he asked.

The emperor heard the child, and everyone began to laugh. The thieves had tricked him! The emperor was not a fool because he couldn't see the fabric. He was a fool for not telling the truth!

Paul Bunyan

Adapted from the American folktale
Illustrated by Gino D'Achille

When Paul Bunyan was a baby, he was the biggest infant anyone had ever seen. His parents spent all day every day finding food to feed him and sewing clothes to fit him. By the time Paul was two weeks old, he tipped the scales at more than 100 pounds!

When Paul finally started to crawl, his booming baby steps caused an earthquake that shook everyone in town right out of their houses!

In fear for everyone's safety, Mr. Bunyan took Paul deep into the woods and found him a cave to live in. He gave Paul an ax and a fishing rod, and said good-bye.

That night, Paul was so sad and lonely that he cried and cried. He cried so much that his tears turned into a giant river that ran all the way to the ocean.

As Paul grew, and grew, and grew he was able to take care of himself with the tools his father left him. Every day Paul chopped wood, caught fish, and explored the forest.

One day, Paul heard a cry from beneath a snow drift. He dug, and dug, and dug until he found a giant baby blue ox.

The giant baby blue ox was so happy to be saved, he instantly became friends with Paul. Paul named the ox Babe, and from that day on, they went everywhere together.

Every day the two friends chopped and hauled enough wood to build 200 houses. Paul knew that folks downriver needed big, strong logs to build their homes, barns, and boats, so he floated every log he chopped to the sawmill for everyone to use.

Because Paul could level an entire forest with one big swing of his ax and a mighty "Tim-ber!" it wasn't long before Paul and Babe ran out of forest to chop along the river. Because they loved to chop and haul logs so much, Paul and Babe decided to find new forests and new friends.

Pretty soon, Paul and Babe found a logging camp full of lumberjacks. No one had ever seen such a big man or such a big ox before, and Paul wasn't used to seeing people so small.

Most people were afraid of Paul, but not the hearty lumberjacks. One day Paul sneezed and almost blew every lumberjack clear out of the forest. Paul was afraid they'd ask him to leave, but instead, one of them offered Paul his bedsheet as a tissue. Paul was extremely grateful for the lumberjacks' kindness.

The lumberjacks were grateful for Paul, too. After a big flood, a swarm of ten-foot bees landed in the forest and stung all of the lumberjacks. The bees buzzed all over the forest until Paul found a boat and loaded it with two tons of sugar. He sent the boat down the river and the bees followed right after it. Paul had saved the day!

For the rest of their lives, Paul and Babe helped lumberjacks float logs downriver. The next time you're in the woods, stop and listen. You might hear the far-off sound of "Tim-ber!" on the wind.

How It Pays Sometimes to Be Small

Adapted from the African folktale
Illustrated by Cathy Johnson

Long ago in a village far away, there lived a beautiful young woman. Everyone admired her and wished to be close to her, especially Sundu, a proud and handsome antelope. One day, the young woman asked Sundu to fetch some honey from a tall tree.

Happy to help the young woman he admired, Sundu found a honey tree and cut a long vine that he would use to hoist himself up to the hive. As big and strong as Sundu was, he could not reach it.

Boloko the ape watched as Sundu tried and failed to get the young woman some honey. Because Boloko also admired the young woman, he decided that he would try to get the honey. But when Boloko climbed up the tree, he did not have the strength to reach the hive. As hard as he tried, Boloko could not collect the honey.

A small mouse in the field had been watching Sundu and Boloko climb the tree. They were both very big and very strong, but the small mouse knew that sometimes being smaller made things easier. The small mouse also admired the young woman, so he decided that he would be the one to climb the tree and bring her honey.

Very carefully, and very slowly, the little mouse climbed up the tall tree to the hive. When he reached the hive, he gathered as much honey as he could carry.

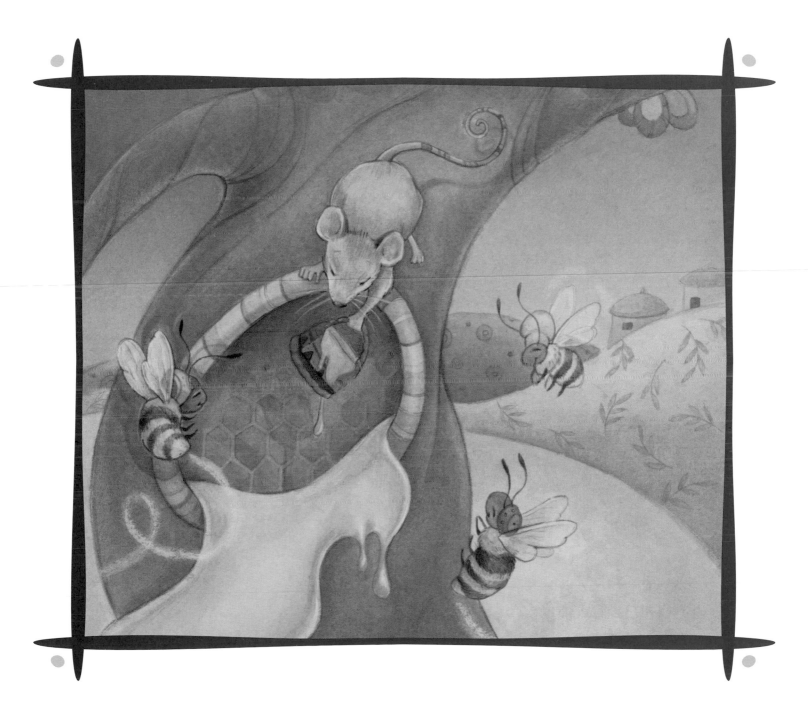

That day a very proud mouse walked into the village with a pot of honey from the tall tree.

"How did you reach the honey at the top of the tree?" asked the young woman.

"It pays sometimes to be small," answered the mouse as he handed her the honey. "Climbing is much easier with less weight to carry."

The young woman picked up the mouse and gave him a kiss. From that day forward, the young woman never needed a big, strong antelope or ape, she just needed her clever little mouse.

The Four Musicians

Illustrated by Wendy Edelson

One day, a donkey overheard his owner talking with another farmer. "I can't find a reason to keep the old donkey around much longer," said the farmer. "He is very old and cannot pull the plow or haul carts. It's time to put him out to pasture."

The donkey could not believe his ears! "Hee-haw!" said the donkey. "I won't be sent out to pasture. I've always loved to sing, so I'll go to town to become a musician! Hee-haw!"

As the donkey left the farm, he saw a sad dog and cat by the road, so he decided to stop and see what was the matter.

"My owner says I am too old to hunt," said the dog. "He's looking for another dog!"

"My owner says I am too slow to catch mice," said the cat. "She is going to get a faster cat."

The donkey invited them to come with him. Together, they would become musicians!

"Mee-ow!" sang the cat in a fine soprano.

"Woof! Woof!" boomed the dog in a deep voice.

As they were on their way, the donkey, dog, and cat saw a sad rooster.

"My owner says I do not get up early enough to wake up the workers," said the rooster. "He says he will find an earlier bird!"

"Join us on our trip," said the dog. "We want to be musicians, and we will need your strong voice."

Nighttime came. The donkey, dog, cat, and rooster had been singing and walking together all day. The rooster began to squawk. "I think I see a light shining from inside a house!"

"They might have food to share," said the dog. "A big, juicy bone sounds very nice."

"I think a big bowl of milk would be *purr-fect*," purred the cat.

"A plate of corn certainly would hit the spot!" crowed the rooster. So the four musicians walked toward the house.

The donkey looked through the window for a few minutes. "What do you see?" asked the cat.

"There are four men sitting around a table that is covered with food," the donkey said.

"What do we do now?" asked the rooster. "Should we knock on the door and ask for food?"

The donkey shook his head. "Remember, we are going to be musicians," he said. "We should practice singing for our supper." The others thought this was a good idea, so they very carefully planned their first concert.

The four musicians decided to stand one on top of the other so that everyone could be heard. Even though the four friends had practiced their singing all day, they were still a little bit nervous. They wished each other good luck, turned to face the window, and cleared their throats.

Never had there been a louder or mightier group effort! The four friends tried to sing better than they ever had before. What they didn't know was that it sounded like "Hee-haw! Woof! Mee-ow! Cock-a-doodle-day!"

The four musicians also did not know that the gentlemen they were entertaining were robbers. They were hiding out counting their stolen gold.

When they heard the loud noise, they looked out the window. They saw what looked like a four-headed beast! "Run! Run! Run!" one robber yelled. "Before the four-headed beast gets us!"

The animals were confused. Why had the men run away? The donkey had the answer. "They loved our singing so much, they must be on their way to find more people to hear our concert."

So the four musicians, believing that it would be some time before the men came back with a new audience, entered the house and helped themselves to the food at their table.

Since they were already inside the house, they agreed it would be best to spend the night there. After all, they didn't want to miss the people who were coming to hear them perform!

Soon their sleepy heads began nodding and their eyes closed. They were all sound asleep when someone tiptoed into the room.

The tiptoeing toes belonged to one of the robbers, who was returning for his gold. He struck a match to light a candle, which scared the cat. The cat jumped up and surprised the robber, who tripped over the sleeping dog. As he stumbled, the robber fell onto the donkey, who gave him a swift kick into the rooster's sharp claws. The robber was so frightened, he ran away and never returned!

The four musicians decided to live out their days in the house. They were very happy giving free concerts and spending all of their new gold.

The Five Brothers

Illustrated by Leanne Mebust

nce upon a time there were five brothers who all looked exactly alike. They lived with their dear mother in a little house beside the crystal blue sea.

The brothers were different from other boys. Their father had been a sorcerer, and they all had special powers.

The First Brother could slurp up the whole sea and hold it in his mouth. The Second Brother could see through the back of his head, and the Third Brother could slip through the tiniest cracks. The Fourth Brother could make himself quite tall, while the Fifth Brother could spin like a top.

When it came time to fish, the First Brother would swallow the sea so they could catch fish. But one day, he did this when the king was trying to swim. The king liked total privacy because he had giant feet, which he tried to hide from people.

The king was very angry when his feet were exposed to the entire village. He ordered his guards to find the person who had swallowed the sea. The king wanted the offender blindfolded and left alone in the dark woods.

The guards found the First Brother and led him to the king. He told the king he had to say good-bye to his mother. The king agreed, and the First Brother asked the Second Brother to take his place. Since the Second Brother had eyes in the back of his head, he easily got out of the woods.

The guards were very surprised when they saw the Second Brother walk out of the woods. They captured him and took the sneaky brother to see the angry king.

The king ordered the guards to lock the boy inside a box. The Second Brother pleaded with the king to let him say good-bye to his mother. He relented, and the Second Brother asked the Third Brother to take his place. This brother, who could creep through any crack, was locked in the box. He wiggled free and scared the guards silly!

The king was angrier than ever. He ordered his guards to take the brother out to the open sea. They were to leave him in the deepest waters.

The Third Brother pleaded with the king to let him say good-bye to his mother. Again, the king agreed. The Fourth Brother took the Third Brother's place and went out to sea. Since this brother could stretch his legs so easily, he was able to stand taller than the deepest water. The guards reported back to the king, who angrily ordered the guards to throw the brother in the dungeon!

Like his brothers before him, the Fourth Brother received permission to say farewell to his mother. He went and asked the Fifth Brother to take his place in the dark dungeon.

Now the Fifth Brother, who could spin faster than a top, knew the floor was solid rock and he needed to go up. He turned and turned, spinning into a blur as he lifted off toward the ceiling.

The king was getting ready for bed when the floor began to shake. The king jumped on his bed as the Fifth Brother spun up through the floor!

The angry king sputtered and spat and declared that the Fifth Brother was a demon!

The Fifth Brother knew he needed to please the king. He looked at the man's giant feet and told the king that he could make his subjects very happy if he used his feet to make mashed potatoes for the entire kingdom!

So the king came to know that he, too, could do things that no one else in the world could do. He was very pleased with his feet. Everyone loved his mashed potatoes and lived happily ever after.

The Birthday Pony

Illustrated by Judith Mitchell

here once was a boy named Philip who had a happy life with his parents and two younger sisters. The family was very excited to be moving to a beautiful home near the town where the children would be attending school. Philip was looking forward to living in a new place and meeting new people.

Philip enjoyed his new school and made friends easily. But he knew that he needed to make good grades because his father had promised him a pony if he did well in school.

The boy received high marks in math and reading but seemed to have some trouble with geography and history. It was hard for him to pay attention. He was too busy imagining all the places he would visit on his new pony. His mind would wander as he pictured himself galloping along the trails as a proud member of the Pony Express.

Philip's father had warned him that ponies were a lot of work. But the boy was determined to prove to his father that he was up to the task. He worked hard and helped build a stable to convince his father that he should get a frisky pony for his next birthday.

"May I please have a pony?" pleaded Philip.

"We shall see," said his father. "Don't you want anything else for your birthday? What about a nice pair of roller skates?"

"A pony is the only thing I want," said Philip.

After that last conversation, his father knew Philip had his heart set on owning a pony. He agreed to accompany him to many nearby stables so Philip could ride the ponies. But his father found fault with every pony the boy liked.

Then a thought popped up in Philip's mind. Perhaps his parents were going to surprise him with a pony for Christmas? After all, his sisters were getting fancy dolls, tea sets, and winter clothes. Philip knew that he had been good all year and deserved a pony to call his own.

Christmas morning dawned bright and clear. Just as Philip expected, his sisters received dolls, clothes, and other things they had asked for.

As they laughed and danced around the living room, the boy felt a pang of disappointment. He had already made a trip to the stable and there was no frisky pony waiting for him.

He dug deep into his stocking and found some money, candy, and a few other things. But they held no interest for him. He had his heart set on a pony, and he had not gotten one for Christmas.

Winter turned to spring and Philip remained blue. He started to give up hope that he would ever get a pony of his own. He began to envy anyone that owned a horse, a pony, or even an old mule. Philip had a very hard time watching them ride past his home.

But something made him turn and look at the beautiful bay pony that came trotting down the street on a splendid spring day. Maybe it was its fine glossy coat. Or perhaps it was seeing that the rider's legs were too long for the stirrups.

The pony's spirited gait slowed as it drew near Philip's home. The tall man got off the little pony and called Philip over. Could it be that this beautiful pony was intended for him?

With his eyes focused on the pony, Philip quickly approached the pair. He did not even notice that his family had gathered in front of the house.

The man looked at Philip and said, "Don't you want to try your new pony on for size, son?"

Philip did not answer. He simply hopped on the saddle and took the reins.

When Philip returned from taking his pony for a ride around the neighborhood, his family was there to greet him. "Happy birthday!" they cried.

"My birthday's not until July," Philip replied.

His father looked at him with love in his eyes and said, "Yes, but we all saw how disappointed you were at Christmas, and we know how much you wanted a pony of your own. So it is an early birthday present from all of us."

Philip rode his new pony into the stable that he had prepared. His dream had finally come true!

Pinocchio

Adapted from the story by Carlo Collodi
Illustrated by David Austin Clar

There once was an old man named Geppetto who had always wanted a son. One day, he decided to take matters into his own hands and carve a marvelous wooden puppet. He wanted his puppet to laugh, dance, play, and turn somersaults just as a real little boy would do.

Geppetto set to work and whittled two feet, two legs, a body, two arms, and two hands. He crafted two twinkly eyes, an upturned mouth, and a tiny nose. But the nose did not stay little.

As soon as Geppetto finished it, the nose began to grow and grow!

"Such a mischievous nose," cried Geppetto. "I will call you Pinocchio!"

Pinocchio turned and winked at the man.

Pinocchio was every bit the boy Geppetto had hoped for, even though he was only made of wood. But just as little boys do, Pinocchio always managed to get into trouble of some sort!

One day, Geppetto gave him a coin to buy a school book. Pinocchio headed for the bookshop — until he saw a puppet show. He used the coin to buy a ticket to the show.

Seeing other wooden puppets, Pinocchio jumped on the stage and began acting foolishly. The angry puppet master told Pinocchio he was going to turn him into firewood!

Pinocchio apologized to the man. He cried because his money was gone.

The puppet master knew the boy was truly sorry. He gave Pinocchio five coins and sent him to buy his school book.

With the five coins jingling in his pocket, Pinocchio came upon a blind cat and a lame fox standing by the side of the road. They told him he should bury his coins so he could grow even more money. Thinking this would help him buy nice things for Geppetto, Pinocchio foolishly agreed. When he returned to check if his money tree had sprouted yet, his five coins were gone!

Pinocchio cried and cried. He had been a bad boy and should have listened to Geppetto.

He looked up and saw a beautiful fairy with golden hair hovering above him.

"Pinocchio, if you really want to be a good boy, you must obey Geppetto and go to school. If you do this, then I will help you," said the fairy.

Pinocchio went home to Geppetto and told him he had been at school. Because he had lied, his nose began to grow! Pinocchio promised to stop telling lies and attend school. But when Pinocchio left for school the next day, he got into trouble again. He ran into a crowd of rough boys. They told him to join them at Playland, where children could do whatever they wanted.

Pinocchio stayed at Playland for an entire year. One day, he woke up wanting some oats and hay. Because he had been so foolish, Pinocchio had become a donkey.

The fairy saw Pinocchio and swept down to help him. She told him she could turn him into a puppet again, but could not take him home. Geppetto was missing!

The fairy told Pinocchio that Geppetto had spent the whole year searching for him. But Geppetto's boat had disappeared into the sea.

Pinocchio told the fairy that he would find Geppetto and never disappoint his father again.

Pinocchio traveled far and wide looking for Geppetto. One day, he saw a strange shape on the shore. He ran toward it before he realized it was a sleeping whale. The whale yawned and swallowed him up!

Inside the whale, Pinocchio heard a familiar voice. It was Geppetto! The two hugged until the whale hiccupped, sending them into the water.

Pinocchio knew that Geppetto could not swim. With great effort, he saved the old man.

After his brave deed, the fairy knew that Pinocchio had a good heart and should be forgiven. As a reward, she turned him from a puppet into a little boy. Geppetto finally had a real son!

The Magic Bones

Adapted from the African folktale
Illustrated by Leigh Toldi

his is the tale of a boy who lived in a hot, dry country. He got sick one day and his mean older brothers left him under a tree. The boy was all alone but made a home there. He built a box to catch food. One day, he found a little old man inside the box. The man gave the boy magic bones so he could make a wish.

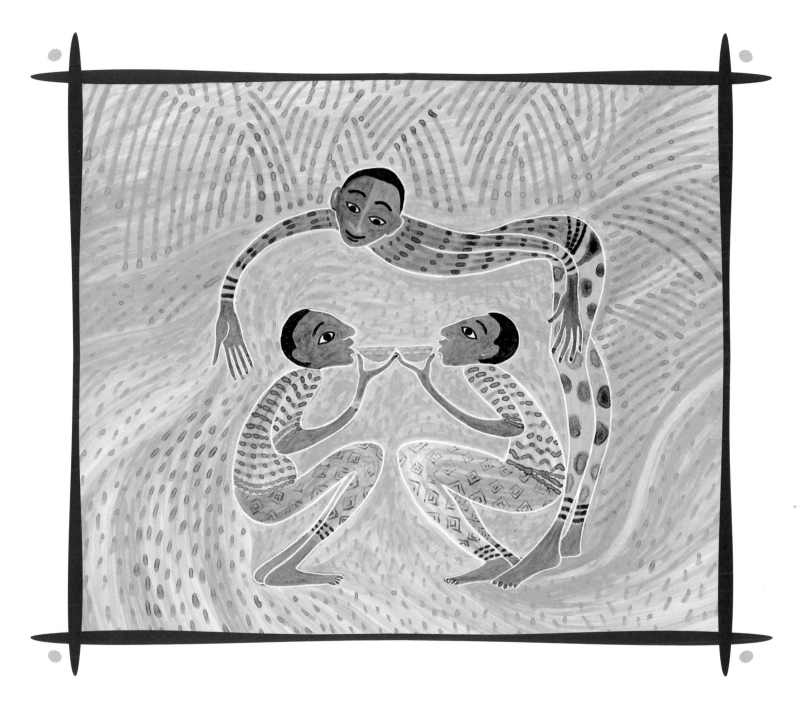

The boy threw the magic bones and a fruit tree shot up. He ate heartily. The old man returned and told the boy he would leave the magic bones with him so he could make a wish anytime.

The boy picked up the bones and threw them in the field. He wished for a large farming village with plenty of food to eat. A village appeared instantly and the boy became its chief.

The boy's brothers heard about this miracle and came to ask the chief for food. He told them he was their brother, and gave them something to eat.

After they had their fill of food, the older brothers apologized to the boy. He forgave them, and invited his brothers to live in his village.

But the boy's brothers soon became jealous. They thought that they should rule a village because they were older. They stole the magic bones and made their brother's village disappear. Then they wished for a village of their own.

The boy cried when he saw what his brothers had done. A rat and a crow came to him. They said they would help him find the magic bones.

The rat and the hawk sped to the brothers' village. The rat took the bones from their home. The hawk swooped down to catch the rat. The brothers believed the hawk would eat the rat.

But the hawk and the rat flew back to the boy and returned the magic bones. He rewarded them by wishing for juicy berries and a plump chicken.

Then the boy threw the magic bones and asked for the return of his village. He also wished that his brothers disappear forever. The village came back to life, and his brothers were never seen again.

The Honest Woodcutter

Illustrated by Tammie Speer-Lyon

here once was a poor woodcutter who lived with his family in a forest far from town. The family often wondered what it would be like to have everything they wanted. The woodcutter tried very hard to provide for his family and wished he could give them more.

The woodcutter headed out to the oldest part of the forest, where the trees grew tall and thick. He sharpened his ax and went to work.

With each swing of his ax, the woodcutter felt he was helping his family. The harder he worked, the more he could provide. He would have to cut down many trees to reach his goal. But his ax was sharp and his strikes were swift.

One day, his family would have a better home to live in, and he would be able to give his wife and children everything they wanted!

Every afternoon, the woodcutter would sit by the river to catch his breath, eat lunch, and have a cool drink. One day, he was very thirsty. He ran to the river for some water and did not see a rock in his path. The woodcutter tripped, and his ax slipped into the rushing river!

"Oh, no!" cried the woodcutter.

The woodcutter looked into the river, hoping to see his ax, but it was no use. The ax was gone. The woodcutter wondered how he would provide for his beloved family.

Suddenly the woodcutter heard a bubbling sound and saw the river rising. A strange figure appeared! It was a water sprite. This fairy of the river had come to help the woodcutter.

"Why are you so sad?" asked the water sprite.

"I lost my ax, and now I cannot provide for my family," replied the woodcutter.

"Don't worry, I will help you find your ax," said the water sprite.

The surprised woodcutter watched as the water sprite splashed back into the rushing river.

The water sprite soon resurfaced. He was holding a beautiful ax! It was solid silver and certainly worth a lot of money, but it did not belong to the woodcutter.

"That is a sharp and powerful ax," said the woodcutter. "But it is not mine."

"Are you sure?" asked the water sprite.

"Yes, I am certain. This silver ax does not belong to me," replied the woodcutter.

The water sprite nodded and dove back into the depths of the rushing river.

The woodcutter watched as the water foamed and swirled. Soon the water sprite returned with a gleaming ax more magnificent than the last. It was made of solid gold! "This must be yours," said the water sprite.

The woodcutter held the amazing ax for a moment. This ax could make him very rich and could give his family anything they could ever want. But the woodcutter could not take something that was not his. He slowly handed the golden ax back to the water sprite.

The water sprite headed down into the river for a third time. When he returned, he held another ax. "That is my ax!" exclaimed the woodcutter.

The water sprite shook his head. "Are you sure you want this ax? The other two are so much finer, and worth much more."

"But the gold and silver axes do not belong to me," replied the woodcutter.

The water sprite smiled and said, "These axes belong to me. But I am going to give them to you in return for your honesty!"

The woodcutter was humbled to be rewarded so greatly just for telling the truth. Overjoyed, the woodcutter thanked the water sprite and watched him disappear back into the water, never to be seen again.

The woodcutter was very happy to have all three axes. He left the forest and headed into town. He would keep his old ax, and try to sell the silver and gold ones.

The shopkeeper marveled at the axes. He gave the woodcutter a large sum of money for them.

The woodcutter went home with a joyful spring in his step and a very happy heart. He could not wait to share the good news with his family. The woodcutter could finally make all their wishes and dreams come true!

The woodcutter's family was so glad to hear that they would have money to buy everything they wanted. But more than that, they were proud he had told the truth. The woodcutter's honesty had been worth its weight in silver and gold!

The Secret Garden

Adapted from the original novel by Frances Hodgson Burnett
Illustrated by Kathy Mitchell

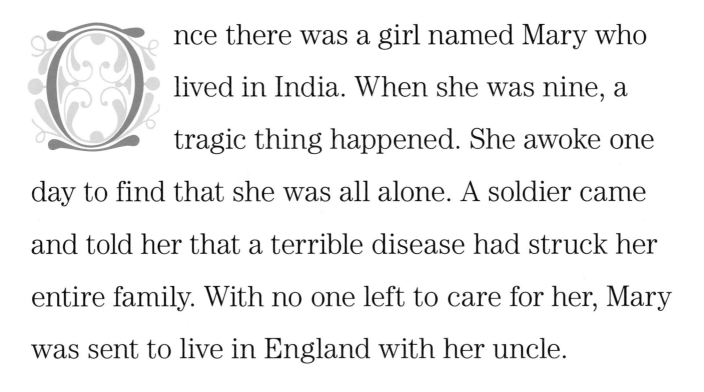

Once there was a girl named Mary who lived in India. When she was nine, a tragic thing happened. She awoke one day to find that she was all alone. A soldier came and told her that a terrible disease had struck her entire family. With no one left to care for her, Mary was sent to live in England with her uncle.

When Mary arrived in England, her uncle's housekeeper, Mrs. Medlock, met her at the train station. As they traveled through the countryside Mrs. Medlock told Mary about her new home. Mrs. Medlock also explained that Mary's uncle, Mr. Archibald Craven, had lost his beloved wife many years ago and did not care for other people's company. Mary blinked away a tear, and stared out at the cold, gray landscape. After living in sunny India, Mary did not think she would enjoy rainy, lonely England.

The next morning, Mary awoke and was greeted by a maid named Martha. Mary stretched and looked out the window. "What is that?" she asked, pointing to the gently rolling landscape.

"That's the moor," said Martha. "It is covered with so many sweet-smelling things."

Martha urged Mary to go out and explore the moors and gardens. She added, "One of the gardens is locked up. Mr. Craven closed it when his wife died, and he doesn't allow anyone inside. He locked the door and buried the key ages ago."

Mary ran outside to explore the green lawns, high walls, and winding walkways of the gardens. Ivy-covered doors led from one garden to the next.

As she stepped into the second garden, she looked for a door leading to the mysterious garden Martha had told her about, but she could not find it. Then Mary saw a gardener gazing up at a little robin in an adjacent garden. She asked him about the secret garden. Just then, the little robin flew toward Mary.

"I think you have a friend," said the gardener.

It rained the next day, so Mary could not play outside. She decided that she would explore the house and look for her uncle's library.

Mary was returning to her room when she heard a fretful, crying sound. She put her hand on the tapestry near her. The tapestry gave way and revealed a secret doorway. Mary was about to open the door when she saw Mrs. Medlock.

"What are you doing?" asked Mrs. Medlock.

"I heard someone crying," replied Mary.

"Don't be silly," said Mrs. Medlock.

The next day dawned bright and clear, so Mary went outside to the garden. Spring was in the air and the earth was beginning to come alive.

Suddenly Mary heard the rustle of little wings. The robin had come to see her. He chirped and pecked at the ground as Mary followed him through the gardens. When they came to a bare flowerbed, the robin stopped to dig in the freshly tilled soil. Mary looked down and saw an old brass key ring. She held it in her hand and wondered if she had found the key to the secret garden.

With the key in her hand, Mary walked along the garden wall, hoping to find a door in the ivy. She decided to carry the key with her everywhere, so if she found the door she would be ready.

One morning, the robin flew over to greet Mary. Then he fluttered to the top of the ivy-covered wall and trilled loudly. At that very moment, something magical happened. A gust of wind rushed down the walkway and parted the ivy, revealing a rusty, round knob. Mary knew it must be the door to the secret garden!

Mary pushed the leaves aside and found the lock. After taking a deep breath, she turned the key, opened the door, and stepped inside. At last, she was standing inside the secret garden. It was by far the sweetest, most mysterious place anyone could ever imagine.

"How still it is," Mary whispered. "I am the first person here in many years."

Mary bent down and began clearing away the tangled weeds and thick brown grass. She wanted to bring the desolate garden back to life.

One day, as Mary was heading out to tend her garden, she heard a peculiar whistling sound. She stopped and found a boy playing music for some small animals. It was Martha's brother, Dickon.

Mary had never played with boys before, so she was rather shy. Mary finally summoned up the courage to tell Dickon about her secret garden. His eyes got rounder and he asked Mary to see it. Mary took his hand and led him to the place she loved so much. Dickon loved the garden as much as Mary did. They worked together every sunny day.

One morning, Martha told Mary that her uncle Archibald wanted to see her. Mary was nervous for fear he would scold her for getting dirty or being in the secret garden. She reluctantly went to the study to meet her uncle.

"Is there anything you want?" he asked.

"May I have a bit of earth to plant some seeds and grow things?" Mary replied.

"Of course, take it from wherever you like," said Uncle Archibald.

Mary thanked him and ran back to the garden.

That night, Mary heard the same crying she had heard before. She got dressed and crept down the hall. She pushed open the door. There, lying on the bed, was a boy crying fretfully. Mary wondered if she was dreaming.

"Are you a ghost?" she asked.

"No, I am Colin Craven," the boy replied. "Mr. Craven is my father."

Mary asked Colin why he did not go outside and play in the gardens. He said he was sick and got tired very easily.

After their first encounter, Mary visited Colin often. The lonely boy seemed to enjoy the lively girl's company. When it rained, they would spend the entire day together. Mary told Colin about Dickon and how he had a way with animals. Then she told Colin about their secret garden.

"You must come see it," said Mary.

"The doctor thinks it's best I stay indoors and get plenty of rest," replied Colin.

"But don't you think that being out in the fresh air would make you feel better?" asked Mary.

One morning, the rain stopped and the sun shone through Mary's window. She put on her galoshes and ran out to the garden. When she opened the door, she found Dickon working in the beautiful, blooming garden.

Later that evening, Mary went to Colin's room to tell him about the garden, but Colin was very upset that Mary had played all day with Dickon. He wanted Mary to spend more time with him.

"I had hoped that my stories about the garden would make you feel better," said Mary.

The next morning, Dickon came to visit with a crow, two squirrels, a lamb, and a fox cub. Colin was wide-eyed. He had never seen animals or talked to another boy in his entire life!

Dickon put Colin at ease when he placed the newborn lamb in his lap. Mary, Dickon, and Colin were soon chattering excitedly and talking about all the fun they would have in the secret garden filled with plants and flowers.

"I can't wait to visit the garden," said Colin. Their stories were making him feel better already.

Mary and Dickon brought Colin to the secret garden. It was the best medicine anyone could ask for. Colin loved seeing all the living things and feeling the warm sun on his face. He spent every day in the garden with Mary and Dickon.

Colin's father returned from a long trip and found his son happily playing outdoors. His wife's garden was alive and thriving again. Not only had it helped a sick boy get better, it brought Mary, Dickon, and Colin together. Their friendship continued to blossom as the garden flourished.

The Queen Bee

Illustrated by Hector Borlasca

Three brothers once were traveling across the land. When they came to an anthill, the two younger brothers wanted to step on it. But their big brother Humble would not allow them to disturb the busy ants. Next they came to a lake where the younger brothers wanted to make a supper of duck soup.

Humble would not allow his brothers to cause any harm to the little ducks.

Later they came to a beehive full of thick, sweet honey. The younger brothers wanted to light a fire beneath the hive so they could have some honey. But Humble told them to leave the bees alone.

Finally, the brothers came to a castle. As they drew near, they noticed that something was wrong. A castle is usually a busy place, with people scurrying about. But this castle was eerily quiet.

"This castle must be under a spell," declared Humble. "Yes," said a guard. "It will be broken only when one completes three tasks."

"What are the tasks?" asked Humble.

"First you must find the three princesses' pearls," replied the guard. "There are a thousand of them scattered in the forest."

The youngest brother thought this would be easy. But he only found one hundred pearls, and was turned to stone.

The middle brother thought he was smart enough to break the spell. He also failed and was turned to stone.

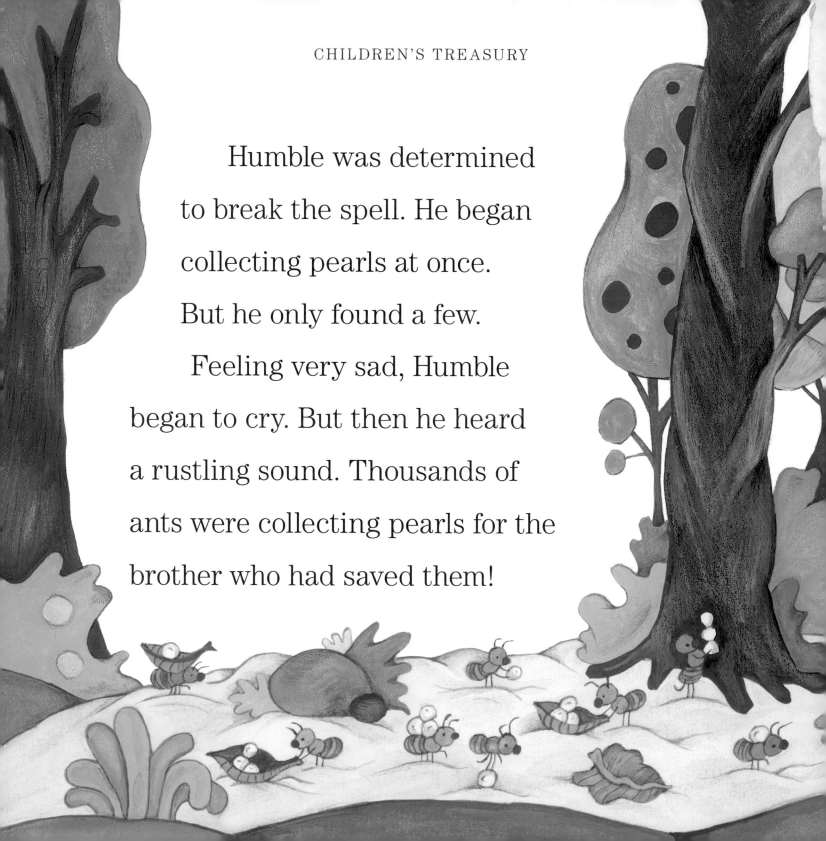

Humble was determined to break the spell. He began collecting pearls at once. But he only found a few.

Feeling very sad, Humble began to cry. But then he heard a rustling sound. Thousands of ants were collecting pearls for the brother who had saved them!

After all the princesses' pearls had been collected, Humble received his second task. He was told to fetch a key from the bottom of the lake. There, Humble saw the same ducks his brothers had tried to catch. They retrieved the key for the brother who had set them free.

Humble returned to the castle with the key and received his third task. He was told that he must determine which of the three sleeping princesses had eaten a honey cookie. Luckily for Humble, the Queen Bee he had saved was there to help!

The Queen Bee quickly buzzed around and helped Humble choose the correct princess. The spell was broken! The princesses awoke and Humble's brothers were changed back from stone. Everyone in the kingdom rejoiced when Humble married the most beautiful princess. Thanks to his kindness, he had everything he ever wanted.

The Fisherman and His Wife

Illustrated by Rusty Fletcher

Once there was a poor fisherman who lived with his wife in a tiny cottage by the river. Every day the fisherman went to the river and fished for their dinner. But one day, he caught a lot more than he bargained for. It was a magical fish who said he was an enchanted prince!

The fish begged the fisherman to let him go, and the fisherman agreed.

The fish thanked the fisherman and said, "I can grant you a wish for letting me go."

"There is nothing I need," said the fisherman.

When he went home, his wife asked, "What have you caught for me to cook for our dinner?"

"Nothing," he said. "I did catch a big fish. But he claimed to be an enchanted prince and offered to grant me a wish. I decided to let him go."

"You should have made a wish," said his wife.

The fisherman went back to the river and called for the fish, who swam to the surface.

"Why did you call me?" asked the fish.

"My wife would like to make a wish after all," said the fisherman. "She wants a nicer home."

"Go home to your wife," said the enchanted fish. "She already has her wish."

The fisherman scurried off and saw his wife waving from the doorway of their new home.

"Now we can be happy," the fisherman said as they looked around their beautiful home.

A few days later the fisherman's wife told him their home was too small, and he needed to go back and ask the fish for a grand castle.

The fisherman wanted his wife to be happy, so he returned to the river.

"Now what?" asked the fish.

"I must ask another favor of you," said the fisherman. "My wife wants to live in a castle."

"Go home. She is already there," said the fish.

The fisherman thanked the fish for granting all their wishes. He trudged home to see his wife.

The fisherman was not surprised to see his wife waving from the balcony of a beautiful castle. But she still was not satisfied.

Early the next morning, the wife said, "We live in a castle. We should be king and queen!"

The unhappy fisherman went back to the river to make another request of the fish.

When the fish appeared, he seemed very angry. "What is it now?" the fish asked.

"I'm afraid my wife wants us to be king and queen," sighed the fisherman.

The waters and the sky appeared to get darker as the fish frowned at the fisherman.

"Go back to your castle," said the fish. "Your wife has become a queen."

Sure enough, when the fisherman arrived at the castle, his wife was already sitting on a high, gold throne. "Now that you are queen," said the fisherman, "surely you will not wish for more."

"I'm not sure of that," said his wife. "I have a feeling that there is something else we need. You might have to ask the fish to grant another wish."

That night the fisherman slept well while his wife tossed and turned in their royal bed.

Just as she was about to fall asleep, the morning sun came up. The wife sat up in bed.

"Husband!" she called out. "I do not think the sun should rise without my permission. Go tell the enchanted fish that I want to have complete power over the rising and setting of the sun."

"Please don't make me go back and call the fish again," said the fisherman. "I fear that this time the favor is too much to ask."

His wife became so angry that the fisherman knew he had to ask the fish for another wish.

Quaking with fear, the fisherman got dressed. He hurried out of his grand castle and headed back to the river.

The fish emerged from the water with a dreadful scowl on his face. "What does your wife want now?" he asked.

"She wants the power to make the sun rise and set," replied the fisherman.

"Enough," said the fish. "Please go."

The fisherman went home and found his wife in front of their humble cottage.

"Husband," said his wife, "I am so sorry I got carried away with greed. But the more I received, the more unhappy I became."

"Yes, we both forgot to be happy with what we had," added the fisherman.

The fisherman kissed his wife and strolled back to the river. It was a lovely day and he was quite content to sit on the river bank. His only wish was to catch a nice, fresh fish for their dinner!

Robin Hood

Adapted from the English folktale
Illustrated by Marty Noble and Muriel Wood

ong ago in merry old England there lived a young boy named Robin Hood. He was the son of a nobleman and had many fine things. His father taught him archery, and Robin became very skilled at it. He practiced every day as his father and the lovely neighbor girl, Marian, watched him.

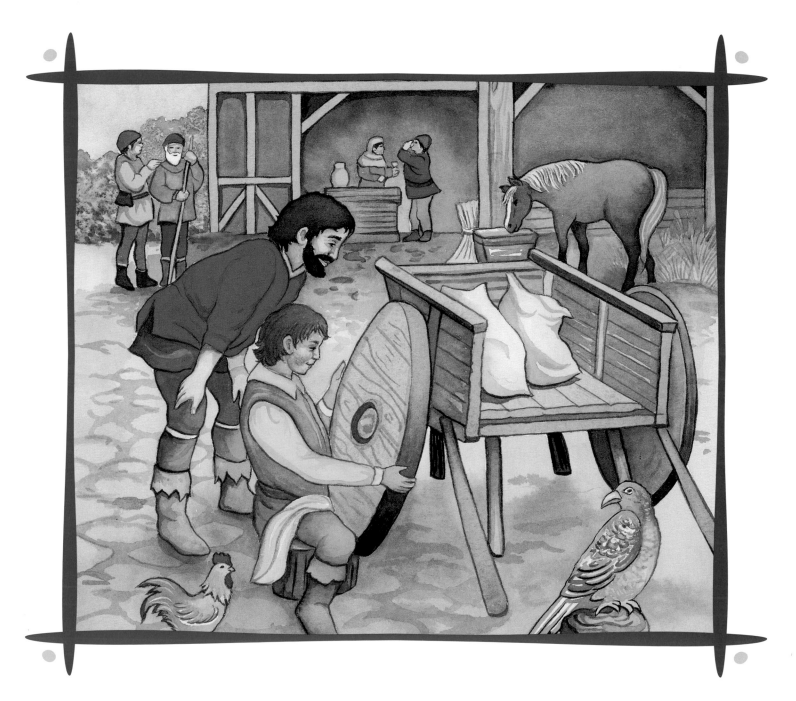

When Robin was twelve years old, his world changed dramatically. His father died in battle and he was sent to live with his uncle. The uncle spent all the family's money, and Robin decided he would be better off living on his own.

The boy had always loved nature, so he went to live in the heart of Sherwood Forest. Robin used his archery skills to hunt for food.

Robin had many friends in the nearby village. They were poor but shared their food with him. In turn, Robin would fix things for them.

When he turned fifteen, Robin decided that he needed to find a job. He set out to join the King's Foresters. They were the men who made sure that the king's property was not stolen or damaged.

The Sheriff of Nottingham did not like Robin and said he was not tough enough to be a forester. He told Robin to kill a deer. Robin refused, saying it was against the law. The Sheriff promised not to arrest him, but when Robin killed the deer, the Sheriff ordered his arrest. Robin's friends outsmarted the Sheriff and helped Robin escape.

Robin vowed that the Sheriff would never trick him again. Meanwhile, the Sheriff was angry that Robin had made him look like a fool. He declared that Robin Hood was an outlaw, and offered a handsome reward for the boy's capture.

Robin Hood went into hiding and befriended many other outlaws. He called his new friends the Merry Men. Because of his archery skills, Robin was named the leader of the Merry Men.

Although Robin was considered an outlaw, he always tried to help the poor people around him.

Now that Robin was the leader of the Merry Men, he set out to right many of the wrongs done by the Sheriff. The men started in the poorest part of Nottingham, where mean tax collectors were taking money from villagers who had very little.

Little John was one of Robin's Merry Men. Despite his name, he was a very big man — so big that when one of the tax collectors saw Little John approaching, he dropped the bags of money he had collected. Robin made each tax collector promise to never take money from the poor villagers again.

Robin and his Merry Men used the stolen tax money to help the poor families of Nottingham. One of the Merry Men, Friar Tuck, insisted on giving some of the money to the church. Robin's cousin, Will Scarlett, helped a family buy food for their little children. Robin Hood gave money to a sick woman to buy medicine.

The villagers were so happy about what the Merry Men had done, they held a huge feast in their honor. "Hurrah for Robin Hood and the Merry Men!" the grateful people cheered.

The news spread far and wide of the Merry Men holding up the Sheriff's tax collectors. The angry Sheriff wanted to capture Robin, so he decided to hold an archery contest.

The contest was too tempting for Robin to pass up, even though he knew it was a trap set for him.

Clever Robin Hood was sure that he and the Merry Men could outwit the Sheriff. They decided to enter the contest in disguise. Robin dressed as a one-eyed beggar and even dyed his beard. He was ready to compete in the contest!

Robin Hood and the Merry Men each came to the contest from different directions, so they would not attract the Sheriff's curiosity. The Sheriff and his men were searching the area for Robin.

Despite being in disguise and only using one eye, Robin was on target throughout the entire contest. Finally it was down to two men: Robin and Hugh o' the Moors. Hugh o' the Moors hit the bull's-eye and thought that he had won. But Robin hit Hugh's arrow, splitting it down the middle. Robin was declared the winner!

The crowd cheered for this mysterious one-eyed beggar as the Sheriff awarded him the golden arrow. The disguised Robin was even invited to have dinner at the Sheriff's home.

Robin accepted the offer and had a wonderful time eating the Sheriff's fine food.

As he was leaving, Robin Hood could not resist letting the Sheriff know who he was. He shot an arrow with a note on it through the window. The note read, "It was Robin Hood who won the golden arrow and dined on your food tonight!"

One day as Robin and his friends were on a walk, they came upon a sad young man. The man said that his beloved was being forced by her father to marry an old rich knight.

Robin asked the man, Allan-a-Dale, to become a member of his band. Allan-a-Dale agreed and Robin Hood promised to help him.

Robin quickly devised a plan to help the man. He gathered up his band of Merry Men and they hurried off to the wedding chapel. They were ready to help Allan-a-Dale marry his true love!

The bishop was about to begin the wedding ceremony when Robin jumped in between the bride and the knight. He said there would be no marriage unless the bride wed Allan-a-Dale!

Robin Hood was ordered to leave. Instead, he called on his band of Merry Men. Little John gave Robin a bag of gold coins, which Robin handed to the bride's father. The old knight saw that he was being used for his money and refused to marry the girl. Friar Tuck performed the marriage ceremony between Allan-a-Dale and his beautiful bride.

One day, as the Merry Men were charging wealthy travelers money to cross the forest, they came upon a potter. Robin Hood demanded a toll and the potter refused to pay it.

"You are no better than the Sheriff to be charging a poor man like me," said the potter.

Robin apologized and agreed to trade places with the potter for a day. The potter relaxed in Sherwood Forest as Robin sold the potter's wares for less than they were worth. Many people bought the pottery, including the Sheriff's wife.

The Sheriff's wife took a liking to Robin Hood and he was invited to the Sheriff's home again. Posing as the potter, Robin misled the Sheriff and told him that Robin Hood had been killed. He even showed him the golden arrow!

The Sheriff demanded to see Robin's body. He was taken to Sherwood Forest and surrounded by the Merry Men. He had been tricked once again!

Robin Hood took the Sheriff's gold and gave half of it to the real potter. The Sheriff's life was spared because his wife had been kind to Robin.

Angry and embarrassed, the Sheriff called upon all of England's top knights to capture Robin Hood. Again, he offered a handsome reward, but only Sir Guy of Gisbourne accepted the challenge.

Sir Guy ambushed Robin Hood in Sherwood Forest. Robin was surprised but quickly recovered. He challenged Sir Guy to a sword fight.

Both men were expert swordsmen and they fought long and hard. But Robin was able to defeat Sir Guy. The knight went back to alert the Sheriff. Robin Hood had eluded him again!

While he was always busy helping the poor, Robin never forgot his childhood friend, Marian. Marian never forgot Robin Hood either. She decided to track him down. She disguised herself so she could travel freely through the forest.

At first, Robin did not recognize the slender, boyish person. But when Marian spoke, all the fond childhood memories came flooding back.

Robin brought Marian back to the Merry Men, and they had a celebration in her honor. The pair soon married and lived happily ever after.

Johnny Appleseed

Based on the American folktale
Illustrated by Rusty Fletcher

here once was a lad known as Johnny Appleseed. He got this name because he traveled all around the country planting seeds so that shady apple trees would grow near people's new homes on the frontier.

Not all the seeds were able to grow, but this is the story about a little seed that did.

One seed fell from Johnny's pack as he walked away from a tiny village with only a few settlers. These settlers had built sturdy log cabins and were hoping to live there a long time. The seed landed beside a little stream in a sunny meadow.

As luck would have it, the soil there was very good for growing trees. It wasn't long before a tender sapling shot out of the ground. Soon the sapling started to look more like a tree. With each passing day, the tree seemed to get a little stronger. Johnny Appleseed would be so proud!

Years passed, and the little sapling grew into a fine tree filled with leaves and apples. Many pioneers passed the tree in their covered wagons. The path beside the tree soon became a rutted road as people continued to head west.

The tree kept growing. Every year it welcomed the newest additions to the deer and rabbit families that came to visit. The tree's branches were filled with quick-footed squirrels and chirping birds. Even its bark was home to tiny, crawling insects.

The friendly tree was glad to have company.

More time passed, and the village became a town. The tree continued to grow, too.

The town was always busy. It was filled with houses, factories, and people. Many of these people chose the big tree as a favorite place for picnics. Whenever there were children around, they always ended up climbing the tree's strong limbs. Sometimes they napped in the shade of the tree. It was the perfect resting spot on a hot summer day. In the fall, the tree's changing leaves made the countryside come alive with color.

One day a big machine came and started digging holes in the ground. The tree heard the workers say the town was "booming." The tree did not know what this word meant.

Soon tall buildings started to spring up around the tree as the once sleepy little town became a bustling city. The old tree grew taller, too. Its branches became thicker and sturdier. Its lush leaves helped shield people from the sun as they went to work or did their grocery shopping. The stately old tree was happy to help them out.

A tall building was built right across the street from the tree. A family with a little boy moved into an apartment there. The boy was sad because he didn't have anyone to play with.

One day the boy stepped over the fence and climbed up the tree. This made the tree so happy! It would hold out its branches strong and still so the boy wouldn't slip. Sometimes the boy would pretend he was a cowboy riding over the plains. The tree became the boy's favorite place. They spent many happy hours together.

One afternoon the boy's mother called him to come in. He did not hear her because he was resting in the tree. The boy's mother was very worried until she found her son sleeping soundly on the tree's large and sturdy branches.

An old man saw the sleeping boy and chuckled because he remembered napping on the tree when he was young. Another woman told the story of how she used to picnic under the tree with her true love. Everyone seemed to have a fond childhood memory of the old tree.

Everyone looked at the tree and its tiny patch of grass. They all agreed that the tree needed to be surrounded by plants, flowers, and greenery.

Someone suggested building a park and all the people cheered. In just a few days, there was a loud rumbling sound again. With the help of the big machines, the people were able to safely move the tree to an empty lot nearby. There, they planted more trees and added swings, park benches, and winding paths. The old tree was very happy in its new home.

Magically, the park seemed to change life for the better in and around the neighborhood.

The little boy had read the story of Johnny Appleseed in school and said that the city should name the park after him. Everyone thought it was a splendid idea.

The little boy continued to visit the tree, even when he was a man with a family of his own. He'd pat the bark and smile up at the tree. When he did, the tree's leaves would rustle happily. The old tree was proud to be rooted in the city's history!

The End